BROKEN BONDS

R. S. CHINTALAPATI

ISBN 979-888555217-2

Dedicated to
Bajju, Mani, Mahi, Milky,
Pakoli, Nikki, PC, Pravi, Chethu, & Nasa.

Contents

Characters

Bhadra - Hero
Rohan - Younger brother of Bhadra
Madhuri - Younger sister of Rohan and Bhadra

Maina - Bhadra's Lover
Sona - Younger sister of Maina

Keshav - Hero
Pallav - Younger brother of Keshav

Neelkanth - Manager of Mind's Quill office.
Nivedita - Keshav's Lover

Pratyusha - Nivedita's friend
Padma - Pratyusha's aunt
Mahesh - Madhuri's lover
Chandini - Maina's friend
Mukund - Pratyusha's Lover

CHAPTER I

Scene I

[This scene takes place in Minds Quill office, a spacious cosy room filled with books on every shelf, a huge office table, and three chairs. They had a balcony where they occasionally smoked. Enjoying the fresh air on a sunny Sunday morning, Rohan and Neelkanth sat facing each other on either side of the table.]

Rohan took a break from reading a novel submission to say:
A good story has a soul within it Neelkanth, and the words were written are to just describe its beauty. The words used in our books are not bad but these books lack the soul itself. Honestly, how many of our recent releases are fascinating?

Neelkanth was also reading another submission. He closed his book, took a deep breath and yelled:
Soul? Let's be realistic Rohan, our writers are getting sold for filmy stories and a majority of our readers are those who expect either violence or sexual content written with vivid descriptions explaining every act! Did you even see our recent sales chart? Our last choice for publishing was the book "Nude'd" and now that is on the top being sold like a freshly baked cake. People are not buying what we expect Rohan. Yes! When we started this business it was very different from what it is now and over the years people have changed. Stories don't get popular unless there is a television show about it or there is something related to sexual content or violence. Readers want pages filled with

great twists. Historical shows and books have now become official sex shows, thanks to the writers.

Rohan putting the novel in his hand aside and closing his eyes mumbled:
Isn't it a disgrace for a writer to fill pages with twists just to grab a reader's attention? Aren't there any writers left to write fantabulous fables that shape the view of children? Neelkanth, every dark act that we publish today shall instil negativity in the minds of our reader's. It pains me when we feed ourselves with the money earned by selling such disgraceful pages. As a publisher I hate myself!

[As soon as Rohan completed his sentence, Madhuri, Bhadra, and Maina enter the room. Neelkanth walked to them as soon as he saw Bhadra]

Bhadra introduced his younger brother Rohan by saying:

Maina, I would like you to meet my younger brother Rohan and that is his friend Neelkanth. Both of them run a publishing house and they are very good at it. I say so because they make profits even in our times when videos are more preferred! My brother also writes but let me just admit it, they are not quite the page-turners that we would love to read.

Maina looking at the crimson red face of Rohan cheerfully said:
So nice to meet both of you. If you don't mind can I ask you why are you so serious? I was told by your sister that your nose looks red but I don't think it is just that now. Why are you so serious?

While Rohan turned to look at Bhadra furiously, wanting to give them some privacy Madhuri interrupted Maina by saying:
Maina, let me show you my home. We could also unwrap all the gifts Mahesh has given me for this Valentine's day. There are loads of them!

[Maina looked at Rohan and Neelkanth for one last time before Madhuri and she left. Bhadra stood looking at the new book on the table and Neelkanth walked along with Maina and closed the door as they walked out]

Rohan slammed the table and shouted at the top of his voice:
You have crossed the line! Tell me this isn't happening! You dare not do this! You will destroy our reputation in our community if you welcome her to our family! Did you forget that she is not a member of our caste! She would be a disgrace amongst our family members and our legacy would be ruined! What religion would your children be off? Being the eldest, you must take responsibility for our family! Look at you!

Bhadra looked seriously at Rohan and said sternly:
Rohan! One more word insulting her and you would regret saying so in the first place. I know you do not wish this to happen and I have thought through it a lot many times! I cannot let go and lead a life as if nothing ever happened. Even if I did, the pain would consume me my whole life. As far as I know, the caste I am born in and the religion I follow has nothing to do with the woman I am marrying. Don't be an educated fool!

[Bhadra walked out as soon as he finished not wanting to hear a word more.]

Neelkanth staring at the furious face of Rohan said:
He is right, isn't he? You are being an educated fool! Looking at you, I see a slave bound to the mortal constraints that we humans built for ourselves. I wish a day would come when men would stand united rather than differentiating each other on the basis of their nationalities, castes, and colour. However, it is hard to accept that a few things will always be dreams after all! Mostly because there are always men like me only hoping rather than striving to make these dreams come true.

Rohan sitting back in his chair stated:
Neelkanth, a day would come when my brother would realize who the educated fool is. The mortal constraints are no foolish deeds, my friend.

CHAPTER II

Scene II

[This scene takes place in the living room of the girl's apartment. To one end was a television and facing it was a sofa filled with cushions and teddy bears. Chandini, Pratyusha sat on the sofa while Maina and Nivedita sat on the carpet filling plates with rice and curry. While Maina just returned back from Bhadra's home, all the others were also exhausted having done window shopping since afternoon. It was a pleasant full moon night.]

Nivedita served rice and asked Maina:
So how did the first visit go? We are quite curious to know what has happened. I wish Madhuri had stayed back, it would have been a delight to listen to her version of the story too. Trust me, I don't understand why she has to leave? If we four girls are staying far away from our families. What would happen if she had stayed back? I get angry when parents insist that their children be back home before 9 PM!

Chandini got down from the sofa and served herself some curry. Tasting the curry, she answered:
It is perhaps because they want to have dinner together! Maybe that is the only time when all the family members meet in the entire day. I seriously never valued my dinner for many years and did not even understand why my mother insisted on my presence but now, I miss my family dinners. Just before I eat, I recall my family. Perhaps Madhuri is lucky to have her family in the same city where

she works.

After a moment of silence, Maina answered:
Yeah, she is kinda lucky. Everything was fine Nivedita and I couldn't meet her mother as she had to travel to the nearby city. Madhuri told me she would be coming back late at night but the funny part was when I met Bhadra's younger brother. You must see him, looks like a joker. Man, the red nose is perfect! He also has a friend named Neelkanth who is quite charming, his dress was amazing!

Pratyusha who was busy with her phone until then suddenly throws it on the sofa and shouts furiously:
What is wrong with this fellow? I told him, I am not interested in a relationship but he never gives up. I told him all about my relationship, still, he says he can't give up on me. He claims himself to be romantic which is idiotic! I will slap him the next time if he keeps on messaging me. Some guys should understand when a girl says no, it is a no!

Nivedita tasted the delicious eggplant curry that Chandini cooked before asking:
Didn't you tell him that you are in a relationship with Mukund? Maybe he doesn't understand what a relationship means. Trust me, it happens... and is it Pallav? If it is him, then you can never make him understand. He has this pre-imposed notion that you and Mukund can't work it out. I don't know what makes him believe that!

Chandini who just finished her dinner continued as fast as she could say:
Even I believe Pratyusha and Mukund cannot work it out. We all have only one soul mate and to think otherwise is

both mad and stupid! I think Pratyusha should be happy that a handsome boy like Pallav loves her. How many boys do these days wait for a girl even after they reject their proposal for a relationship? But still, he loves her no matter what! He is to be admired as these are the days when relationships are like contracts agreed by two people! Love is not a clause in it, unfortunately.

Maina heard Chandini and asked curiously:
You were right about the madness but why would a girl like a boy who is already in a relationship? Isn't it foolish if she is giving herself to a boy who actually loves another girl with her knowledge? Are these girls we are talking about real? Because, if my Bhadra would someday love someone else, I would kill him! He is mine and only mine. That is how it is and that is how it should always be!

Chandini was shocked on hearing Maina, she never expected that Pratyusha didn't tell them about Mukund:
Seriously? Both of you don't know that Mukund actually loves another girl apart from her? Come on, guys! You never knew that? I thought you knew it. She loves him despite the fact that he actually loves another girl! Whenever I ask her, she tells me that he told her, he loves her more than the other girl! Their whole relationship has been like this since the beginning!

[Maina's face turned pale. She did not believe what she just heard and was lost in her thoughts]

Nivedita furiously asked:
Pratyusha! What is wrong with you? Do you love Mukund even after he loves another girl? You are not only fooling

yourself but you are also destroying the other girl's relationship! My God! How can you even do this? Did you even think twice before taking this decision? Boys lie all the time and if he is just lying imagine how much that would affect you!

Pratyusha snapped back:
Nivedita, you out of all should not talk about relationships! You don't even have the courage to accept Keshav's request. It has been two years since he proposed and even today, he is waiting for a response and you are talking about love? Frankly, nothing can be more amusing!

While Nivedita was grinning her teeth unable to say anything Maina said:
Alright! I have been in a relationship for years. Am I qualified to tell you? Just because a boy says, he loves you more, it isn't true! Loving a boy who loves two girls at once is as foolish as it sounds and the worst part of it is that you are defending your actions! Pratyusha, it doesn't take a genius to tell that you are fooling yourself. You would end up either breaking another relationship or sunk in sorrow about a boy whom you believed! Ultimately, you would regret letting him betray you!

Chandini clapped in excitement and shouted:
That is exactly what I told her in the first place! I told you, he would leave you if you force Mukund to choose between one of you. He is just having fun and you are letting him! Why don't you just start afresh and love the boy who loves you? He is lovely!

Pratyusha burst out saying:

None of you know the pain of letting go of a boy whom you love wholeheartedly! You talk so much about soul mates Chandini? What if your soul mate loved another girl? Would you just let him go? And Maina, if your cute little Bhadra loved another girl, can you just wipe off your memory and forget him? All of us are the same! We are selfish but we preach when it isn't our fault. I am not fooling myself and if you were in my position, none of you act any different!

The room was silent for a few moments and breaking the silence, Pratyusha said:
I am sorry guys. For me, this is very personal and I understand you guys are trying to knock some sense into my head but it would take time. However, I promise that I will ask Mukund to choose and Chandini, if you like Pallav so much, why don't you start a relationship with him?

Chandini stated:
Pallav and Me? My god! He is younger than me. He is like my little brother!

CHAPTER III

Scene III

[Finishing his work on the first day of the week, Keshav returned home tired. Working in a steel company was very tiresome and for a graduate who has only a year of training, it was tough. Fortunately, he got placed on the outskirts of his hometown and was living with his brother. Keshav visited his family every weekend and as he rested on his unorganized bed filled with clothes, his younger brother Pallav knocked on the door before entering. The sun was setting.]

Pallav looking at his brother sleeping on the bed in his formal dress said:
Brother, can I talk to you for a few minutes. I am stuck in my life and everything seems to fail. My job is boring, my love life is in a mess, as the girl I love is with another. I want to learn a few tips from you and before you say anything, I would like you to know that you are my inspiration for many things. It takes a lot of determination to stick to a girl who doesn't respond to you when you are in love with her. I value you now more than ever because I feel it. There is nothing more disheartening than a one-sided relationship!

Keshav sat and was surprised to listen to his brother's admiration towards him. He asked:
Pratyusha didn't give up on Mukund, did she? My little brother, since you have come to me for help, I am being completely honest with you. I don't know how determined you think I am, but you must learn one important thing

today. Two people love each other only when they can be happy and see a future together. At the end of the day, it all comes back to happiness and no matter how we see, all healthy relationships are those which are filled with happy moments outnumbering the sad ones. However, to start one such relationship there is one crucial element that both the boy and the girl should share. It is called hope! No matter how determined a boy or a girl is when his or her partner doesn't have a hope of a successful future, the relationship would not even begin but if they really share hope, I believe it is the inception of the trust! Over time, this trust would make their thoughts alike and every moment with his or their partner would be bliss!

[Pallav loved what he just heard. He was so surprised that it was all so simple when his brother says it]

Keshav continued after Pallav sat beside him on the bed: But, not all relations are the same as this world has millions of minds living together. Sometimes, few people actually build their hope on wrong persons but they wouldn't know it, would they? This hope is a slow poison as it doesn't just kill the individual's happiness but would make them question the concept of relationships. I am sorry for saying this but both you and Pratyusha are hoping for the wrong persons, she is hoping for Mukund which is never going to happen as he doesn't share an ounce of hope with her and you are hoping for her which would also not happen because if she realizes her relationship won't work, she would be devastated. Which means she would in no way even think of starting a relationship with you.

Pallav thought for a second and asked:

I don't understand why doesn't she sense he is using her? Everything is plain and simple! Why can't she just open her eyes and see what exactly is happening? Am I asking too much? Or is she is being foolish, isn't she? What is so difficult to understand?

Keshav was fed up but he took a deep breath and explained:
She isn't being foolish, please stop saying that and also stop wondering why she is not liking you but try to understand why she is still hoping for Mukund. She is not letting it go because deep inside, she has hope. Do you even believe that without an ounce of hope, I stayed with Nivedita for such a long time? She is hopeful about our future as much as I am! You would be a fool if you still hope for Pratyusha!

[Pallav did not say a word.]

CHAPTER IV

Scene IV

[It was sunny friday afternoon and just a few hours before the weekend holidays started, Neelkanth and Rohan waited for the author in their office. These meetings were conducted to seal the deal about royalty that would be paid after the book was published. As the clock short hour hand reached four, Nivedita arrived and knocked on the door.]

Neelkanth opened the door and welcomed her:
Hello there, my name is Neelkanth. Nice to meet you in person Ms. Nivedita. We are pleased to sign a deal with you, I was fascinated reading your manuscript. I must admit that it needs a bit of editing but my God you are excellent at playing with your words. Please take a seat and this is my brother and publisher Rohan!

Nivedita greeted and settled down in a chair while Neelkanth gave her a glass filled with grape juice. Sipping it, she said:
I am glad you guys liked the story. Though it might sound rude, I must also admit that you guys have a different taste as compared to other publishers to whom I have sent it to previously. Some of them even lost their taste for tragedies and every paperback book I buy today is filled with stuff that would rush the adrenaline. Being a reader, I sometimes feel that just because the writer wants the character to be a hero, he is made to look like one but none of his qualities inspire me and just don't ask me about the heroine. She is just a supporting character in most of the novels these days.

I have recently read a book titled "Nude'd" and trust me, it was suggested to me by three of my close friends and every word in it is shit! My friends enjoyed the lead female role getting drunk, partying late night, dating random boys for sex and what not! Given a chance, I would punch the publisher straight on his face for publishing such a piece of garbage!

[While Neelkanth smiled, Rohan smirked looked at him. A moment later]

Rohan leaned forward and spoke for the first time saying: Then, you can just punch me on my nose and scold me as you wish because I am the idiot who published it. Forgive me; I regret publishing it more than you do but sometimes we don't have a choice, do we? I believe for a publisher to publish one good book, he has to publish at least ten bad books filled with stories that readers would love to read. If not the publisher would have no business to run or investment to publish another book. Anyway, I found your book quite captivating and I find your views quite impressive too. Business aside, would you like have a cup of coffee with me sometime?

[Neelkanth was shocked seeing Rohan asking a girl to him join for coffee]

Nivedita smiled and replied:
I wouldn't mind at all. Shall we meet at 6 PM?

Nivedita stood up and left with hoping to complete the business talk that evening.

Neelkanth walked along with her and closed the door. He immediately turned back and shouted:
What the fish! What just happened? Did you ask a girl out for coffee? Rohan, is everything alright? I feel like my world has been just ripped apart. It is like an unexpected catastrophe! Did you like her by any chance? Man, I am going to kill myself today!

Rohan smirked again.

He knew that it has been years since he asked a girl for a cup of coffee but after Neelkanth kept on shouting in excitement, he replied:
Come on Neelkanth. Look at her, she looks beautiful and let alone her beauty, her views about valuing family more than friends, her way of writing words and arguing about the various elements of writing is impressive. What more could I seek from a girl to ask her to join me for a cup of coffee? She left me curious and now it is the time I learn about her as much as I can.

Neelkanth heard everything patiently and replied:
There was once a friend of mine who told me, "Even the most idiotic works in writing have something of an essence imbued in them and all that it takes is to look at them from the perspective of which the writer intended us to see it from" and that idiot is just staring at me now. When you talk to her, I am afraid of what might happen Rohan, as you seem quite impressed by her already.

After a moment of silence while Neelkanth and Rohan looked at each other, Neelkanth continued:
Rohan, do not make a mistake, Gods' aren't cruel but they

wouldn't hesitate to test every one of us wanting to see if we would really live up to what we deeply believe in our life!

Rohan smiled before exclaiming:
And Gods' would be amazed to see me answer them!

CHAPTER V

Scene V

[This scene takes place in Mahesh's apartment at 4 PM on Friday evening as the sun was setting. The room was cleaned by Mahesh as soon as he received a message from Madhuri well in advance that she would be coming to meet him. In the past, there were times when Madhuri left as soon as both of them reached his place, as Mahesh seldom cleaned it and the apartment stinks. After she arrived and both of them settled down, Madhuri sat on the bed caressing Mahesh's hair and he lay on her lap.]

Mahesh looked at Madhuri as she was lost in her thoughts. He asked:
You seemed to be distracted. What happened? Are you getting those horror dreams again or are you wondering about our future as you always do? You must understand that I am settled and will take good care of you. I am a member of your caste by the good grace of all Gods and your mother has no reason to reject me. Don't worry about me being eight years elder than you, I think your mother wouldn't worry about that either as back in her time, even a gap of ten years was nothing.

Madhuri looked at Mahesh for a moment and replied:
I am not worried about us. I am worried about my elder brother and Maina. After many arguments, Rohan failed to convince Bhadra to let go of his relationship with Maina for the family. Two days back, they had an argument again and Bhadra just walked away calling Rohan a fool it seems. My

mother isn't the woman most of my friends thinks she is. Though she appears to be calm, she is not! After we lost our father, she has taken both roles and I have never seen any woman of her age being more stubborn than her. I know, for sure, she wouldn't even allow Maina to step into our kitchen and imagine my elder brother wants to bring Maina as her daughter-in-law. I am worried about what would happen!

Mahesh smiled before saying:
I believe you are overthinking it. Most parents wouldn't let go of their children, especially mothers. For them, their sons are the most prized possessions and the last thing they would do is to let them go! Don't worry. Nothing will happen. In fact, I am sure your mother would compromise and welcome Maina gladly as a member of your family. She is a good girl and is beautiful. What more could your mother ask for? She might not be of our caste but she is from a royal family after all! I don't see any reason why your mother would not be convinced.

Madhuri was disappointed as Mahesh did not understand the seriousness, so she shouted:
You don't understand Mahesh! Maina isn't that perfect and I don't blame her. No girl of her age is perfect, do you think I am perfect? But the problem with Maina is quite different. She is short-tempered and I can't even imagine what would she say in an argument that would inevitably happen when she would meet my mother? I dread the thought of both of them fighting. Bhadra cannot pick a side! Neither Rohan nor I can handle the situation.

[Mahesh did not want to talk about this topic, so he

diverted the discussion saying: Say whatever you want to about Bhadra but I like him. Your brother has got the guts to stand up for what he believes and loves in his life. I think Rohan lacks that, thanks to your mother. He is as stubborn as she is and I am afraid he might suffer a lot in the future!]

Madhuri hit Mahesh on his head and said:
And that is why I say you are crazy! You praise the family idiot and forget to even acknowledge the hero!

CHAPTER VI

Scene VI

[After many calls, Mukund finally messaged back to Pratyusha that he would meet her in the Casting cafe they usually meet at. As the sunset, Mukund and Pratyusha sat facing each other after ordering two cappuccinos and a chocolate pastry. The waiter brought them the coffee and pastry]

Mukund sipped the cappuccino before saying:
So finally madam, you wanted to meet! What is the matter? Miss me? I know it has been a long time since we met but I think this meet is for a specific reason. So, before I start expecting great things and imagine loads of stuff that actually never happens, please tell me why you wanted to meet me?

Pratyusha looked at Mukund staying silent as she did not know where to start, however, a moment later, she said:
Mukund, all this time you have been telling me that you love another girl as well but as days pass by, there is this question in my mind that pops up asking what is our future together? All this time, I waited in hope that someday you would bring up this topic but you never did. So, I want to know now what is our future? Have you ever given a thought about it?

Mukund tasted the cake and started smiling as soon as he heard the word future. Mocking Pratyusha, he said:
Look at you! You talk like you an about to be a married girl

now! We are just twenty-three and there are many years ahead of us. Planning the future is done by fools who can't live their present life. Don't worry, I am no fool as I rejoice to live in the present. I rejoice every moment of it and my only goal is to earn as much money as I can. I believe in "Live the moment!" so don't ask me stupid questions like having you thought about our future? Our future? Puff! If it makes you feel any better, my answer to your question is I have never even thought of my future.

Pratyusha was disappointed but she was determined to know given the choice whom would he choose, so she asked:
Mukund, can you seriously answer me one question? I am confused about my life and please don't make fun of me this time. I want you to listen very carefully. If you were to choose between me and Ritika, whom would you choose to lead your life with? Don't you dare just say my name without meaning it, as you would have to leave Ritika forever and stay with me if you do so. I think I have been fooled enough just by hoping for great things from you! And you have been enjoying my lenience! Today, things must be cleared once and for all!

Mukund lovingly asked:
What happened to you all of a sudden? I have been telling since the very beginning. I love you more than her. Why don't you just listen to me? We had great times in the past and I see us...

Pratyusha interrupted by shouting:
Don't you try to beat around the bush again! Don't tell me that you love me more and all that bullshit! Answer my

question, if you have to choose between both of us, whom would it be? I am seriously not going to ask you again and you dare not joke again with your stupid answers. Just say is it me or her!

Mukund looked at Pratyusha's stern face. He looked all around, he knew this day would come. Giving up on whatever might happen and unable to look at her, he closed his eyes before he said:
Ritika it is!

[He expected to be slapped or water being thrown on his face but nothing happened and when he opened his eyes, the chair before him was empty.]

CHAPTER VII

Scene VII

[At 6 P.M., Rohan left to the nearby Casting cafe to have a cup of coffee with Nivedita. He was excited to know more about her as her ideas resembled his ideas. For some unknown reason, he was admiring her without even knowing her completely. Saying goodbye to Neelkanth, he walked to the nearby Casting cafe and Nivedita was already waiting for him.]

Rohan greeted her and after both of them settled down and ordered, he started:
So, before I ask you about other things, we are willing to pay sixty percent of the royalty to your book. I hope you are convinced with the deal and if you are convinced, we would be delighted to welcome you to the community of creators! I hope, you would contribute many such books in the future to our publishing house. However, before the release itself, I am letting you know, always remember that books and movies are very different from other forms of art in terms of reception from the readers or viewers. Over the years, I am sure you would also know that. Sometimes, people love them even if it they are simple and sometimes, they won't even pick them up even if it is super fun. None of us ever understand how it works!

Nivedita thought about the deal for a moment and accepted saying:
Thank you for the deal. I am glad, my first work is getting finally getting published years after I finished writing it

and please don't worry about the reviews. For a person like me determined to tell more stories, I think reviews can do nothing but motivate me to write better. Anyway, I would like to know why is that you asked me to join you for coffee? I am sure this isn't the usual thing that you do with all writers whom you sign a deal.

Rohan smiled as the waiter served them coffee. He frankly wanted to tell her why he invited her, so he said:
Let me cut to the chase. I invited you for a cup of coffee because I wish to know if you truly believe in a few things that you have mentioned in your novel. Frankly, I find them quite interesting because I also share the same views. For example, the lead role in your novel given a choice between family and friends chooses family. Her priorities are fixed and she doesn't even have second thoughts! Do you share the same view or is it just for the story?

Nivedita immediately answered:
I share the same view as well. Isn't it foolish to actually trust your friends more than your family? You depend on your family for almost everything but wouldn't even care to share something important? Such things make me go crazy! I seriously don't understand why friends share their darkest secrets with others but don't talk to their brothers or sisters. It doesn't make sense to me, how do they trust their friends so much? These relations can fail instantly and sometimes the friends we trust are the ones who turn against us, aren't they? As a famous author once said, "The only person who can hurt us the most is the person we loved and trusted!"

Rohan was amazed. He loved the way she said it. He said:

Exactly! I totally agree with you and can I know...

Nivedita interrupted him and Rohan was a bit taken back but wanted to listen to what she had to say:
I am sure you know that I am one of your sister's friends and I would like to know your opinion about my friend Maina and your brother Bhadra being a couple? I want to know because I have heard a lot many things about you. I have heard, you talk about family legacy and believe in the caste system. What surprises me is, being an educated graduate, you support the caste system which actually divides the country! I am sorry for asking this but only since you asked my view, I am in return asking yours.

Rohan finished his coffee and said:
Alright. Do you know why everyone around me really thinks I am an idiot? Because they have in their mind, the image of me dividing people and setting priorities for everyone based on their caste and religion but the reality is I don't do that. I simply oppose inter-caste marriages because every caste in India has its own way of living. When a couple is from two different castes, there are many aspects that wouldn't go hand in hand and compromise is the only way. Now, you have said a great deal about trust, tell me, would you purchase an item knowing for a fact that you would have to compromise on a lot many aspects using it? Hell no! None of us do unless the item is itself a rare possession. But, look at my brother, he is making a choice in which he would have to compromise on many aspects for a lifetime! I believe he would regret this decision somewhere down the road in the years to come. I feel, he would reap what he has sown now.

Nivedita smiled listening to Rohan and wondered how Madhuri boasted about him. A moment later, she explained:
From what I understand, you don't even know what love means! When you say Bhadra has to comprise, I say it doesn't really matter if they are from the same caste or from a different caste. It is all the same as leading a life with another person would always require someone to compromise and seriously do you really think all of that even matters? You need to understand that at the end of the day it all comes back to one thing, looking into the eyes of each other and letting our hearts shout out in joy that they love each other. They believe that no matter what happens, there is another soul in this solitary world who loves them. I strongly believe that there is nothing more beautiful than the warmth of a lover's hug and the bliss in a kiss!

Though Rohan wanted to argue interrupting her, he heard everything patiently. Later he said:
Alright, let's just say I agree with that. What about my brother's legacy? I assume you know that when the castes were initially created, it was based on the nature of work and the human mindset. For example, Brahmins are more into acquiring knowledge while the Kshatriyas are brave and ferocious. This division was not meant to divide the humans but was to make the proper use of the inner potential of a person. If a talented child is denied education, it shall not only affect him but in fact would affect the whole society and in today's world, unfortunately, there are thousands of children being placed into something that they are not meant to be in and look at our society now! What has happened over the years was that the caste system was differently interpreted. Maybe because the

majority of us started honouring jobs involving mental activity rather than physical activity. This honouring of specific jobs has created a differentiation that destroyed the whole purpose of caste creation. Over the years, even respect for hard workers like farmers has decreased and now we live in a society where children are forced to attain a white-collar job! Only if they do so, they are respected! A society bound by the rules of caste is successful and progressive as most of the children would use their inner potential to help the society but as days pass by, these inter-caste marriages are staining the legacy our forefathers have left for us. I would never accept the legacy, my forefathers passed on, getting stained. I respect Maina by all means and she is always welcome to our family as a friend but not as a relation!

Nivedita was tired. She knew arguing with an adamant guy like Rohan was of no use. So, she curiously asked:
And what would you do if someday you would love a girl who is not a member of your caste? Would let her go because she would stain your legacy?

[Rohan looked at Nivedita and smiled]

CHAPTER VIII

Scene VIII

[Around 9 p.m., Chandini, Nivedita and Pratyusha settled around the dining table exhausted. They cooked mashed potatoes curry and made chappati, cooked steamed rice to eat with pickles and curd. As they settled down and waited for Maina, she messaged Nivedita that she would reach home in ten minutes.]

Chandini mocked looking at the serious face of Pratyusha by saying:
What did your soul mate say, Pratyusha? Did he choose you? Did he promise to stay with you for a lifetime? Or did he just make another false promise again?

Pratyusha stayed silent and Chandini continued:
None of us would ever understand the value of what we have until we lose it. Yes, we always are stuck with the wrong person but we must learn to grow over it and start fresh again. I am glad at least today he told you the truth!

Pratyusha looked at her phone and stayed silent. Nivedita was fed up with Chandini and wanting to change the discussion, she said:
I have never seen such a crazy guy who is so obsessed with his religion and caste. I find him quite curious and frankly, it would be great to learn more about Rohan as guys like him are rare to encounter in our daily life and I do not wish to miss the fun.

Both Chandini and Pratyusha did not care about what she said and Chandini again started blabbering. So Nivedita shouted:
Stop being so harsh on Pratyusha! At least she did not lock herself in a room sobbing!

Before Chandini said another word, the door opened and Maina walked in. She threw her handbag and crashed on the couch. She shouted looking at her friends:
I am never going to their house again! What does she think of herself? How dare does she shout at me and call me headstrong! Anyway, there is no point in cursing her now. I have put myself in such a position! I loved a fool and now I am to obey his mother's commands as well! She looks at me from top to down and it made me feel like she has no value for me. Whenever I tried to talk, she wouldn't say a word. Once in a while, she would just say a word randomly and she did not care of me being present with her trying to obey her! I don't understand what does she even think of herself? Even my mother has never been like this! Not even when she is angry with me! The worst part is my future husband sits with his little brother in the living room and does nothing! And when Madhuri tried to say something, her mother would give her a stern look! Lastly that joker of the family! I don't know what is his problem! Can't he even fake a smile for my pleasure when I look at him? Does it cost him a fortune?

For a few moments, everyone was silent and Nivedita broke the silence saying:
You knew beforehand that it would not be a welcome party! On the brighter side, you did not have an argument I suppose and that is such a relief. Trust me all the three of

us were worried if you would come back after a fight. With your short temper, you could have set a lot of things into action but thank the Gods nothing of that sort happened. I am glad you did act foolishly.

Maina's expression changed and looking at her Chandini shouted:
My God! She had an argument! You stupid girl, can't you even control yourself in the name of God! Every time we tell you to control yourself, you ask "Why should I?" You defend saying that you wouldn't get angry without a reason! Now you better tell us a good reason for getting angry!

Both Nivedita and Pratyusha looked at Maina curiously wanting to hear what happened and Maina explained:
Yes. We had an argument but listen before you judge. After repeated attempts of trying to talk to Bhadra's mother, I could not as she was least friendly. However, after a while, she asked me to make some tea.

Nivedita, Pratyusha and Chandini's expressions changed. They all knew the taste of Maina's tea. Maina stopped for a moment waiting for her friends to hear her out and continued saying:
I did make some tea. I even offered it to everyone and after tasting it, Bhadra's mother did not even say a word. Though Bhadra said it was tasty, the joker and Madhuri said nothing. My sweet mother-in-law took a deep breath and asked me if I knew how to cook. This time I wanted to be truthful and told her, I could cook a few dishes and I also told her that I am willing to learn but before I concluded my sentence, she furiously asked: "Did your mother teach

you anything?" That sentence made me so furious too and I couldn't control my anger any longer. I shouted, "The same thing you taught your daughter!" I even asked her to honestly tell me, "How would she feel if Madhuri's mother-in-law would treat her the same way as I was being treated? Why couldn't she consider me as her daughter? She shouted back saying, "You dare not raise your voice against me!" And I slammed, "I don't care if you are offended but I wouldn't live in your house as long as you can't respect and consider me as your daughter!" As I left, Bhadra tried to talk to me and I asked him to choose between me and his mother and left!

Nivedita and Chandini still stayed silent as they knew saying something would not change anything but Pratyusha spoke for the first time asking:
You asked him to choose between his mother and you? You are a monster!

CHAPTER IX

Scene IX

A week later

[This scene takes in Pratyusha's aunt's living room. After making her son sleep, Padmini arrived to talk to her niece in the living room. They sat on the sofa facing each other leaning on the cushions. The television was switched on and muted in the background.]

Padmini asked looking at Pratyusha:
So tell me what happened? I was definitely sure something was wrong when you messaged me if you could join me for dinner tomorrow. It has been a year since you started staying in the city and this is the first time you met me after you arrived. I am definitely sure something isn't right. What is it? Is everything alright with you and Mukund? Or did you and your friends have an argument? Is everything alright at work?

Pratyusha answered:
Everything is alright at work and I did not have an argument with my friends but Mukund and I broke up. Aunt, before you say anything, I want you to know that I am not sad about it as somewhere within me I felt someday this would happen. I have come here today to just spend some time with you and ask for your help.

Padmini hesitated but asked:
What happened? Why did you guys break up? I thought

everything was perfect. Did he do anything wrong?

Pratyusha did not wish to tell her aunt what exactly happened. She did not want her to again point out that it was her fault. Looking at her, Padmini said:
Alright. Doesn't matter what went wrong. I am sorry that things did not work out. So what is that you are bothered about?

Pratyusha finished her apple before saying:
Father is sending me messages asking me to get married. Just after we broke up, he even asked me if there is a boy I liked so that he could talk to him and decide to get me married. I said I have no one I like and now he is insisting that I get married since there is no one I love anyway. You know it is tough for me, unfortunately, I am unable to even accept the thought that someone else would take Mukund's place by marrying me. What do I do now?

Padmini understood her niece's problem very well. Sooner or later, most girls end up with the same problem but she knew no solution. After a few moments of thought, she answered:
I am very sorry but I really do not have an answer to what you have asked. I always thought that you would get married to the person you loved the same way I did but never did I think that your relationship would break. However, I want you to explain to yourself and accept the fact that sooner or later someone else would marry you and you should love him and lead a life with him. If you cling to the person whom you loved, life would not seem attractive because even every pleasant and cheerful experience would make you dissatisfied because your mind would

remind you about missing the person you love.

Pratyusha argued:
So you want me to just forget him? I can't. I planned my entire future with him and he just walked away as if he did not care for me ever. He might have not loved me but I loved him and no matter what I tell myself, it wouldn't change my love towards him. He would always be the person I adored.

Padmini agreed:
Yes. He was the person you adored and he would have made all your dreams come true but he did not wish to lead a life with you, I am sorry but you must respect his decision and let it go. We all dream great things and if our dreams don't come true, we must be in a position to accept it. I am not asking you to forget him, I know it is tough to do so and even after trying you might fail but you must understand that your life is more precious and every day you spend trying to forget him is just a day wasted. My advice would be, do not forget him, just try to accept that it is all over.

Pratyusha nodded her head agreeing and her aunt continued:
Just try to make yourself understand that you being happy is of paramount importance than anything else now. Is that clear?

Pratyusha said in a sad voice:
Yes.

Though Padmini felt bad for her niece, she could not do anything else. She said:

Most of us love the wrong person but that definitely does not mean there is no one else in this world who could fill that void. Time heals everything and you will be perfectly alright.

CHAPTER X

Scene X

A week later

[It has been two weeks since Maina last met Bhadra. He tried talking with her but she would not listen. Neither Madhuri nor Rohan could help and in evening, Rohan called Madhuri sitting in his office and as reached, she could see her brother getting ready.]

Looking at her, Rohan asked:
Are the situations getting any better? Has Maina given up on her stupid decision of not coming to our home and apologising? Tell her that problems should be solved but not enhanced and just saying a sorry wouldn't destroy any of her reputation. She can consider our mother to be hers and apologize for once. I think everything would be fine and if she gets lucky, our mother might be convinced to welcome her back into the family!

Listening to her brother Madhuri seriously asked:
Tell me, brother, if in the future, let's just say after I get married, I have an argument with my mother-in-law and even though I have said nothing, should I be the one who should apologize? Would you want your sister to be sorry for nothing while my mother-in-law does not even respect me or our family?

Rohan smiled and without a second thought said:
Without a doubt, I would say, you should apologize. As it is

important to solve the differences and stay together, not to fight and defend your respective arguments. If a five letter word could solve the problem, I would say there is nothing wrong in saying it repeatedly until the problem is solved. I don't think that is such a great deal? Both of them had a stupid silly argument and our mother is a bit stubborn. She wouldn't even dream of apologizing to her daughter-in-law, so why not the other way around?

Madhuri was fed up to even ask another question, so she stayed silent and Rohan continued:
Anyway, I have called you to ask something that is very important. In the past few days, I have been meeting your friend Nivedita and she is really a wonderful person. Trust me, I frankly couldn't admire anyone more! But there are a few things which I would like to know before I meet her today. The first thing is she in a relationship?

Madhuri was amazed as soon as she heard relationship but she pleasantly answered:
She is not in a relationship but brother where is this going? Don't you dare surprise us! You of everyone knows that our mother cannot take another blow! Just yesterday, she talked to me about Maina and her only problem with her was the caste. Personally, our mother has no problem with Maina but she is worried about what our relatives would think. She cried leaning on my shoulder complaining about how her elder son is making her suffer! I always believed that you would never hurt our mother. So please don't create...

Rohan put on his coat and simply interrupted saying:
I think you need not worry! I wouldn't disappoint our mother and great things are going to happen today! Wish

me luck!

Before Madhuri spoke one more word, the door opened and Neelkanth walked in. Saying bye to both of them, Rohan left.

Looking at Madhuri, Neelkanth said:
My father always told me that when a man is about to either achieve something great or ruin everything, he would be in a rush. During this rush, he neglects all the hints and suggestions that he receives thereby becoming a slave to his hope but the bittersweet reality is that it is the failure that will embrace him most of the times! I have never seen Rohan rushing in his life like this and personally, I am very happy for him. But I fear for your mother maybe because it is the innocents who always suffer while the foolish shall always rejoice in their ignorance!

CHAPTER XI

Scene XI

[Returning back from work in the evening, Keshav washed his face and made some coffee and took a box filled with biscuits. He settled on the sofa and checked his messages while sipping coffee. Enjoying every moment of it, he was about to open the box of biscuits when the bell rang. Putting his phone on the table, Keshav opened the door to see Chandini.]

He was surprised to see her:
Chandini! Come in. It has been a long time since you have come here. Looks like you have become too busy managing the sales representatives and I see many of them in the locality these days. Anyway, what brings you here all of a sudden? To what do we owe this surprise visit?

While Chandini sat on the sofa, Keshav gave Chandini the second cup of coffee which he made for Pallav.

He passed her the biscuits and thanking him, Chandini said:
I have come to talk to you about something very important about your relationship. In the past few days, I think Nivedita has been quite busy meeting a guy called Rohan. Of course, she has been meeting him to get her first book published but I personally think she is starting to love him. I am not backbiting and have only taken the effort of coming here to tell you that. It is very important that you know about this since you loved her for a long time. I am

warning you beforehand!

Keshav sat stunned hearing what Chandini said. He looked at Chandini in disbelief and did not know what to say.

After a few moments of silence, he shouted:
Chandini, what is this? I thought you and Nivedita were good friends. How can you even say that about your friend? Haven't you got any respect for her? I trust her and not even for a moment would I believe what you are saying is true! This is disgraceful on your part!

Chandini smiled looking at Keshav. She could not control herself looking at her foolish friend.

However wanting to still help him, she replied:
Disgrace? Seriously? That is what you are telling me? You have been in Nivedita's friend zone for years giving her the utmost respect. Believe me, when I say, nothing is greater for some girls than having boys friend-zoned. Your loving Nivedita is the queen of such girls! I have come all the way to help you and you are calling what I did as disgraceful? Do you know what is disgraceful? Loving a person who can't even say to her friends that you are her boyfriend! I was there when you proposed and here we are two years later. Tell me what changed? I have never heard her say once that she loves you, neither did I hear her say you were something more than a friend. But here we are talking about disgraceful acts? Call her right now and ask if what I said isn't true and if it is not I will never ever raise a word about your relationship and even apologize to her.

As soon as Chandini finished, Keshav became furious and

took his phone and called. As he called, he walked out to the garden.

As soon as Nivedita picked up her phone, he said:
Hello Nivedita, can I ask you something very important?

Picking her handbag and adjusting her hair, Nivedita answered:
Hey Keshav, I am quite busy right now. I am going to meet my publisher. Anyway, I wanted to talk to you about something very important too. Can I call you after a few hours? Because I am already late and Rohan told me that there is something very important that he wants to talk to me about. He would be pissed off if I go late unlike you.

Controlling his anger Keshav shouted:
Nivedita! If you cut this call, as you always say "Trust Me!" our relationship ends here and now! I am not going to tolerate this any longer. Unless you answer my question, if I were you, I would not cut the call!

Nivedita was aghast and Keshav continued:
Good. Now there is something I would like to ask you honestly answer. But before that, you need to understand that I am not asking you this out of suspicion but out of fear of losing you! Even though all these years we were separated, I never felt lonely but for the first time, I feel like, I am all alone. Are you in love with Rohan?

As soon Nivedita heard Rohan's name, she took a deep breath. She was not able to say a word. Though her mind said to her to just shout, "What the hell is wrong with you Keshav! He is just my publisher!" but her love for him did not let her lie.

Frankly, she did not love Rohan but she would be lying if she said:
"She did not have any feelings for him."

After a long silence, Keshav asked in a broken voice:
This has gone too far, isn't it? If you have to choose between one of us, who would it be?

[While he wished, he heard his name, Nivedita did not say a word and a moment later, he just cut the call]

CHAPTER XII

Scene XII

[This scene takes place in the Casting cafe. Nivedita arrives and Rohan is already waiting for her.]

As soon as Rohan sees her, he says:
I was thinking about leaving. You are late as always, so what good reason do you have this time?

Looking at her worry about something, Rohan continued:
I see you are wondering about something and I wish that it is about your next novel. No one would be happier than I am to read one more fantastic work by you. However, today there is something I would like to tell you and I would love it if you would pay your full attention!

Nivedita was thinking about Keshav. She recalled the day he proposed to her and she regretted not even lying. When Rohan asked her to pay full attention, she started paying attention.

Rohan took a deep breath before saying:
For many years, I believed in legacy and caste. I stood by it supporting my arguments every moment in my life until I met you. Only then, did I realize that to have a life filled with happiness, it is not the religion or the caste that matters but it is the thoughts that matter. I was so glad, I finally found a girl who could think just like me and what pleased me the most is your priorities. There was not even a day when I thought that I would be so happy to propose

to a girl and start a relationship until I met you. Kaboom everything changed! I see in you myself, a twin! I see a future in bliss and to start this wonderful journey, all I ask of you is approval. Trust me when I say, you have moved me so much, that I have even let go of the philosophies I believe in just to be with you. I would defend us by fighting against everyone who comes in our way.

Nivedita sat silent. She thought for a few moments while Rohan had coffee. After Nivedita made up her mind, she said:

A few weeks ago, I met a man in the very same place we are sitting now. He said a lot many things about life, caste, and religion. He even opposed his own brother claiming that he has brought upon his forefathers legacy a stain but the irony is, the same person who held great things once is now stating that he would compromise on everything he ever believed in. You know what, there is a word to describe a person who preaches but doesn't follow and it is called a hypocrite and there is a hypocrite sitting before me now. He even wants me to join him.

[Without saying another word, Nivedita stood up and walked away. On her way back, she wiped her tears. Rohan just leaned back and his eyes were filled with tears]

CHAPTER XIII

Scene XIII

[This scene takes place in a Shiva temple. After his darshan, Bhadra sat on the stairs leaning on a pillar looking at the peepal tree before him. He thought how his father could have helped in his situation and closed his eyes for a few moments. As soon as he opened his eyes, Bhadra's father sat beside him.]

He was amazed and before he said a word, his father said:
I always thought my elder son was strong in taking his decisions. Looking at you for the last one month made me wonder if I was wrong in estimating your capability. I never thought my son would be stuck in life without peace about simple issues. Tell me, what is life if not taking proper decisions and I believed like every other father that my son would be wise enough.

Bhadra asked in a sad voice:
What do you want me to do father? No man should ever be put in my position. I am being asked to choose between my mother and the girl I love. Is it fair to be forced to choose between them? Tell me father what would you have done?

His father did not take even a moment to answer:
I would have chosen my mother. The question at hand is not to make this choice, the question you must now answer is, "Do you think this girl is the perfect choice for a lifetime?" These are times when people change their course of choices within days and are you sure that this girl is the

perfect one?

Bhadra immediately said:
She is my world and she is everything I ever wanted for. Yes, she is the perfect one. My life would be bliss if she is with me.

His father smiled while Bhadra wondered, he said:
I was also once your age and I was just like your brother. Foolish, adamant about caste, religion and legacy. I married your mother without knowing anything of what a marriage really meant. Over the years, I understood that it meant an event to establish formally that two people are willing to bond and share responsibility. After you were born, I understood that marriage was something more important than just responsibility. I understood that it was a promise that two people made. A promise in which they would share their happiness as much as they would share their sorrows.

Bhadra pointed out:
We too share our moments' father. We help each other out and she knows the best of me as much as I know the best of her. I mean it when I say, she is the best person I know after you and mother. Is it too much of me to ask to share my life with her? Is too much to welcome her to our family?

While Bhadra questioned, his father questioned back:
Is it too much of your mother to ask you to give her the freedom of choosing your partner? Is it too much of her to expect her daughter-in-law to be obedient? I would not say what Maina did was wrong. She is too young and I would not expect anything more from her than defending

herself but what I could not tolerate is that she asked you to choose. No man should ever be asked to choose and if asked to do so. Something is terribly wrong either with the woman he loves or the woman who has given birth to him.

Bhadra accepted:
I agree father but she was angry. She has her own reasons. She says if your mother is so authoritative before marriage, I would definitely not be happy after marriage. I cannot live with her as long as she is authoritative, what would you have me do father?

His father said:
You said she was your life, I believe in my son and let her prove that you are also everything to her. Tell her that if she wishes to marry you, your mother would also be with you. Tell her that you cannot be irresponsible just for your love.

Bhadra hesitated to do so as he was worried if Maina would not accept. Looking at his son, his father assured him:
She would agree son. She loves you too. Initially, she might hate it but over time she would get along with your mother and everything would settle down. Consider this as a test of time and face it bravely. If you qualify for this test, you shall become capable of writing your own future.

[Bhadra opened his eyes and his father was no longer sitting beside him. He looked at the tree for one last time and left]

CHAPTER XIV

Scene XIV

[This scene takes place in Mind's Quill office. Neelkanth finishes reading the first draft of the story that Rohan forwarded to his email.]

Neelkanth impatiently shouted:
I think you must stop writing for some time! I don't know what exactly happened between you and Nivedita but that incident is having its impact on your writing! Three sex scenes and the heroine dies in the end? This is definitely not the work you usually deliver and just because a girl did not accept to your proposal, you should not kill your lead character! This is insane and in your terms, this story lacks one thing the soul itself!

Rohan laughed. He knew Neelkanth would oppose it:
Soul? I don't think it needs a soul. Let's just put it out there and the readers would make it a classic. There is nothing more beautiful than making the hero weep standing before his lover's grave. If people like stupidity, I am ready to deliver it. Don't you forget that there are many successful story books out there, let me just write one and put it out for people to read! I am just making it realistic and Nivedita has nothing to do with the ending. If you believe that a girl's rejection would have had an impact on my ending, I think by now, I should have written many books quite differently!

Neelkanth slammed:
Rohan, I really want to know what happened between you

and Nivedita. I am not curious but I am definitely concerned! Knowingly or unknowingly, she pulled the trigger for your self-destruction and looks like this is the just the beginning! Look at you, you won't talk to your brother. You won't meet any authors to sign deals and now you give me this script to publish? Man, I am seriously worried!

Rohan leaned on his chair. Both of them stared at each other for a moment before Rohan shouted:
Neelkanth, don't blame Nivedita! I have come up with this story long before I met her and she has nothing to do with the ending! Don't you worry about me and it would better if you don't indulge into my personal matters! I don't recall asking you what your cute Aparna told you when she rejected your proposal? You are just here to help me with the publishing. Get it done!

As soon as Neelkanth heard Aparna's name he looked into the mirror that was to his left resting on the wall. His hair was neatly combed, he wore a light blue formal shirt. Before he said anything, Neelkanth took a huge breath.

He knew what he was about to say would affect his relation with Rohan seriously but he did not hold back:
I am sorry but I would not publish this script and destroy your reputation. I would rather leave this business than print this script. This would destroy your reputation and for me it is everything! You are not just my best friend but also my best writer! I look up to you and expect to reach your level when I am writing my short stories and I will never publish this script!

Rohan's nose turned red. He shouted:
Get out! You are fired! I don't want your valuable advice on my writings! I can sell my own books! I fed you and thought of you as my own brother...

Neelkanth interrupted to say:
I am your brother.

Rohan continued:
Not anymore! Apparently, you can't trust anyone in this life. My own brother can't decide if he should be responsible, the girl I love calls me a hypocrite and my best buddy judges one of my best work to be soulless! I can't take it anymore, get out!

[Neelkanth stood up and without saying a word walked out.]

CHAPTER XV

Scene XV

[This scene takes place in Pallav's room. It is early in the morning and Chandini comes to Pallav's home at his request. They sit in his room.]

Looking at him, Chandini asked:
Still can't get over Pratyusha? I think you are one of your kind. I have never seen a boy like you, all of my friends get into new relationships as soon as their existing ones fail but look at you still stuck in the past. I have spent hours talking to you to let it all go and I don't know how else can I help you. I can't convince Pratyusha because she apparently does not care about anything and Mukund took good care of her by shattering her heart into a thousand pieces!

Pallav sighed:
I have called you here not to talk about Pratyusha but I have something more important to tell you. The last time we met, you talked a great deal about how I understood Pratyusha very well and personally I did not recognize that fact for myself. After a lot of thought about all that you spoke, I have understood that you have in fact cared about me more than her. All she ever did was wail about Mukund but you have stood beside me and made me realize... You took good care of me!

Chandini's eyes widened as Pallav continued:
As many authors wrote in the past we all love the wrong

person and I am sure, I did that as well. I sought a girl who was in love with another but never cared to observe my friend who understood me more than anyone else. So now, I would like you to know that, I am not telling you this because I am looking for a partner but I believe no one else understood me like you apart from my mother!

[Chandini was aghast. She could not speak though she wanted too and Pallav concluded saying: I love you and would promise you that if you share the same affection towards me, I would never let you down all my life! I have taken this decision after a lot of thought and I personally don't care what others think. What matters ultimately is to be with the person who understands you in the best way possible!]

Chandini took a deep breath before shouting:
How dare you take advantage of my friendship? I have always cared about you as a friend and here you are proposing? Are you seriously asking me to be your life partner! Do you even know when I was born? Do you know my tastes? Just because I supported you when you were hurt in a relation, it doesn't mean you can propose and take advantage of it!

Pallav was about to say something but Chandini continued:
Perhaps this is all my fault because I was supporting since the beginning, this happened. If I would have cut you off at the beginning itself this day would not have come. Aren't you ashamed to propose to me after you loved my friend? Have you an ounce of dignity? If I say no would you now go and propose to Maina? Is this like a game?

Pallav shouted:
Will you shut up! This is not a game and I have dignity! Just because I proposed, it doesn't give you the right to scold me as you like. You can just say no and let it go! I have proposed because never in my life did anyone else understand me as much as you did and I don't think it was for nothing. Please don't talk about being ashamed as there is nothing to be ashamed of and I just proposed because I share a feeling!

Unexpectedly Chandini heard Pallav out before mentioning:
But you are younger than me and I have never even imagined you to be my boyfriend. My God! I should have been careful since the beginning! After giving it a bit of thought, I think I should blame myself as this has happened only because I have taken too much care! I should have taken care of my own business! Sorry, Pallav! But you have crossed the line and taken advantage of my support! This is very bad and there wouldn't be a day I would not regret thinking about this!

[Chandini stood up and left. Pallav took a deep breath and thought it was just a bad idea to even express his views. He left to work that afternoon and just before he slept in the night, his phone buzzed and the message read "Do you really love me?"]

CHAPTER XVI

Scene XVI

[This scene takes place in Maina's room. She took a vacation to meet her family on the occasion of Diwali. After a day full of shopping, she slept beside her sister Sona as they always shared the same room since childhood.]

Sona was curious to ask what happened when Maina met Bhadra's mother because she knew nothing more than that it did not go well. While she was in a dilemma as to whether ask or not, Maina questioned:
How is your relationship with Arjun? Is everything alright or is it like a sinking ship like mine?

Sona could not help but ask:
What happened between you and Bhadra? I am really curious to know what happened? Both of you were very good together and he was fantastic company. You know how our father initially had second thoughts but over time, even he knew that Bhadra was perfect for you. So what happened?

Maina thought about the first time Bhadra met her father. Perhaps, she had never been tenser in her life as she wanted her father to be impressed. As she was recalling, Sona asked again:
What happened sister? We have always spoken to each other about the various issues in our lives, can't we share this? I might not be helpful but at least I can share your pain.

[Maina told her sister all that had happened and how Bhadra had met her before she was came home to say to her that if she was willing to marry him, it would be a family along with his mother.]

Sona patiently heard every word her sister told and was confused. She thought, whatever she just heard was a very simple misunderstanding. So she asked:
Sister, do you remember what father asked when he met Bhadra for the first time? He asked him why he should allow him to marry you. I was listening to their conversation and in this conversation, they talked about various things if I recall correctly. They talked about how much money Bhadra would be earning, they talked about the future Bhadra had in his mind for the both of you and honestly, I have never heard or seen our father be more serious while asking questions in my entire life.

Maina snapped:
Our father was concerned about me and he wanted to make sure that Bhadra was the guy who is appropriate as my life partner but Bhadra's mother was not concerned if I would be a proper partner. She was provoking and wished that I start an argument! She knew her son would take her side and so started this argument.

Sona hesitated before saying:
I think you are taking all of this from the wrong perspective. No family member especially parents would be willing to welcome a new person into the family without giving them a hard time. They would like to how this person would behave in different circumstances. Just as

an example, if Bhadra was asked how much does he earn and as soon as he answered if our father points out that it is nothing and questions him how would he take care of himself earning so little leave along with you. Let's just say if our father asked that, do you think Bhadra would immediately argue with our father because he felt insulted?

Maina admitted:
He would not...

Sona continued while looking at her sister realize:
I am sure Bhadra is not perfect. If that is the case, none of us is but we all settle with the person with whom we believe our lives would be worth living even though we are compromising in many aspects. Perhaps that is what love is all about, isn't it? I might be younger but this is all that I know. You and Bhadra had your differences and before things get out of your hands, settle your differences and just be a bit patient for a while. Maybe the future is more beautiful, who knows?

Maina smiled. She looked into her sister's eyes before asking:
Where did my little sister learn all of this from?

Sona blushed before answering:
It is one of the perks of having a boyfriend who writes and fantasizes about stuff that usually motivates people to be stupid rather than being rational.

CHAPTER XVII

Scene XVII

[This scene takes place in Neelkanth's home. Madhuri visits to invite Neelkanth to her marriage. Though Mahesh wanted to come, she wanted to meet her brother alone. After welcoming her and offering her coffee and cakes.]

Neelkanth said:
Thank you for coming. It means a lot to me and how is Rohan doing? I have read good reviews for his new book. I think this world has a good taste for entertainers rather than artists. Frankly, no one would be happier if his book doesn't perish against the test of time and he gets back with his life. The last time we talked, he seemed impatient.

Madhuri replied:
One of my friends screwed up everything! She has a big mouth and apparently did not think twice before calling Rohan a hypocrite when he proposed and that moved him to his core. He has been working on books continuously ever since and I don't even know if he is getting any rest. I talked to him yesterday and he told me that he fired you after you had an argument. So I have come to talk to you about coming back, my brother might not realize your value but without you, his works don't mean a lot many things that they meant in the past. I must admit that I love his work now, however, I think with your guidance, the works would be valued forever.

Neelkanth smiled as soon as he heard the words "valued

forever". He said:
I am flattered but I think we are beyond repair Madhuri. I believed in him for years! But when he said, I was not his brother, I was hurt. Words are powerful and what pained me was that he did not consider me as his brother. Maybe, I hoped too much. I thought he was my family and believed in every one of you and it pained me when he said I was not.

Madhuri had no words to say. After a long silence, she stated:
No matter what happened or happens, you are always a member of our family and without you, we are incomplete. So I am requesting you to please come back and let things fall back in the place where they previously belonged. Two of my brothers are already suffering thanks to my two friends, please heed my request.

Neelkanth thought about it for some time before answering:
I will come back when Rohan invites me personally. Me coming back now wouldn't help change anything. I can just walk in tomorrow and apologize to set things straight but that would not help. Let Rohan take his time to come back to his conscious and maybe then, I can come back. You need to understand that the day when Rohan started the publishing house with me being a partner, I promised myself that the day when I am no longer counted in terms of my views and opinions, I would walk out of the company. Unfortunately, the Gods have heard it too well, I guess. They made it happen.

Madhuri eagerly asked:

So, if my brother would welcome you back, you would not mind coming back? That could be arranged. I will speak to my brother and make it happen.

Neelkanth objected as soon as Madhuri finished:
Don't. I don't think Rohan would need help. He would sort his way out. Anyway, there is something I want you to do. I want you to give him this manuscript, tell him that this is my first drama and it is based on real events.

Madhuri questioned taking the booklet:
What is it called and on whom is it based? Can I read it before I give it to my brother? Can I read it, please? I promise that I would never talk about it after I read it. I find dramas are always quite fascinating to read.

Neelkanth knew what he was getting into, so he thought about his sentences twice before he spoke:
I have no problem if you read it but do not be angry with me of what is written in it. I am not sure if I should be glad or cautious to say that even you are a character in the drama. It is based on our family, friends and it is a collection of a few incidents that mean a lot many things teaching the audience the choices or decisions we make or take might not be perfect but we could work it out.

Madhuri was amazed as soon as she heard, she was also a character. She shouted in enthusiasm:
I don't care even if you oppose me from reading as I am going to read it anyway. Writing a drama based on real characters is not easy. Maybe, because these real characters might force the writer to stick to their decisions even when the writer has better ideas at every point in the plot.

Neelkanth knew that many scenes he had written might seem childish in terms of a third person but as a real experience, he knew most of the choices made were based on the characters real choices.

He admitted:
Yes. You are right. I thought in many instances of why a character would take such a choice even when everything is laid out before him. It made me understand that none of us values the decisions that others make unless it seems to be great from our perspective but we seek a lot of support for every decision we make.

Madhuri recalled as soon as he heard the word perspective:
I have one more good news. Madhuri & Mahesh are getting married two months later. I hope everything would become normal by then. I was so happy when my mother accepted my request. She had her doubts but soon Bhadra and Rohan helped in making her believe that it was a good match.

Completing her sentence, she passed the invitation. Neelkanth cheerfully congratulated before hugging her.

CHAPTER XVIII

Scene XVIII

[This scene takes place in a park near Nivedita's apartment. She called Keshav many times after he cut the call the last time when he asked her a question. After many days he finally replied to her messages and she requested him to meet her. Both of them sat on a bench beneath the tree in the shade.]

Nivedita started the conversation by saying:
Keshav, before you say anything, I would like you to know that I am very sorry about what has happened. That incident made me realize many things and I have called you here today to tell you what I really feel about you.

Keshav in a low voice said:
I hope you just don't tell me that I would get a better girl because I definitely am not looking for another! Moreover, tell me honestly what were you thinking when I asked you if you were in love with this Rohan? Three years Nivedita! Three years! I spent nights, many nights with sad experiences and my only hope was that one day, I would hear from you that you love me and all I got was silence! Life really taught me a good lesson!

Nivedita shouted:
Would you listen to me? I have come here to tell you that I do have feelings for you and every day just as you hoped, so did I! But for some reason, I was distracted! I promise you from this moment that I would share your happiness

and misery. I would stand beside you lending my support as you once asked me. I am sorry it has been a long time but some things never get old and you are always my lover boy! I agree Rohan distracted me but he definitely made me realize your value! I wonder what would I be without you!

Nivedita could see Keshav blushing. This is the first time she has seen him like this and he was adorable with his dimples. As he looked at her, she kissed him.

Keshav opened his eyes to say:
You are quite unexpected if you know what I mean and are you sure that you love me? Or am I just hallucinating? Because I don't really know what reason I should tell myself to feel sad tonight. I have been accustomed to being sad rather than rejoicing.

Nivedita smiled before telling me:
Hope that you convince my parents as well! Honestly, convincing them is more difficult than convincing me. Given that you took three years to convince me, I think you would definitely be successful in getting their approval within five years! If you know what I mean.

Keshav raised his eyebrow and proudly boasted:
Well, I am the bridegroom and if there is anyone who should be convinced, it is me. Anyway, how much dowry would I get to marry you?

Nivedita laughed, Keshav concluded saying:
Well that was worth a try!

CHAPTER XIX

Scene XIX

[This scene takes place in Pallav's room. Chandini visited him to sort things out after talking to him through the phone for many days.]

After a long silence since she arrived, Chandini spoke:
Pallav, I have come here to tell you a secret. I initially wanted to tell it to you through phone but I felt it would be much better if I tell it in person. While we were in our bachelors, I loved a guy and I am not making this up just to avoid your proposal. He was our teacher and the feelings were mutual. Over the years we stayed in touch and even now I love him. I am very sorry but I cannot accept your proposal and moreover, you are younger than me.

Pallav was curious to learn why she kept mentioning the word younger. So he asked:
Chandini, why do you keep on saying every time that I am younger to you. It sounds like you are reminding yourself that you should not start a relation. If you just don't have the feelings, why don't you just say a no and let it go? Why do you have to tell me about our teacher? Why do you have to ask me if I truly love you? Why do you have to talk to me every day? Accept it or not, I think you share an affection but I feel you are letting it go. To just stay resolute on your decision, you are repeating the same reasons again and again!

Chandini initially smiled but soon snapped:

That is not true. I talked to you every day just to make things clear and I am telling you are younger because that would really affect if we start a relation! But above everything, I am already in love. I hope you understand. Moreover, I am going back to my hometown to attend an interview, I got qualified for a government position in the written exam and before I leave, I wanted to let you know that it was great to have such a good friend like you since Bachelors. My life would have been very different if you were not a part of it. However, all that I can say is that you would get a better girl than me and I wish you stay happy.

Pallav was sad, he wanted to ask for one last time:
Chandini since you are anyway leaving. Can you just for once tell me the truth? Did you ever love me? I would never ask you again and this topic would end here and now. Please tell me the truth.

Chandini smiled and kissed on Pallav's forehead.

As she took her bag, Pallav shouted in excitement:
My brother was right. Hope is a monster! I would even stay single all my life if I would not win your heart!

[Chandini laughed as she left]

CHAPTER XX

Scene XX

[This scene takes place in Rohan's mother's bedroom. While he lay on the bed, his mother sat leaning on the headboard of the bed reading a book. It was a cloudy evening and cold air managed to enter through the open windows.]

Looking at radium paint on the ceiling, Rohan asked:
Mother, if I am not interrupting, can I ask you a few questions? Perhaps in the last few days, I had been through many incidents and I want to learn what is the way I must choose from all these incidents. You alone can answer these questions in the best way possible.

His mother closed her book and taking off her reading glasses asked:
What is that you have been through?

Rohan skipped the question to ask:
I was wanting to know if a person should choose his caste over his lover or lover over his caste? By caste, I mean marrying a person in the same caste to keep his future generations pure. This decision-making process is so conflicting that I was not able to come to a conclusion of what to do. I thought it was a simple decision but situations have taught me that it is not. We don't get to choose the person we love but we only get to only choose the person with whom we lead a life. What do we do when we love someone and they are not from our caste?

His mother answered:
If it is love against caste that you are asking me about, I would prefer caste but that is my choice and it does not mean that I must enforce it not even on my children. At the most, I can advise but you must understand that all of us have different priorities and not everyone believes in keeping their bloodlines pure. Some say marrying the same caste person would not make us pure unless our thoughts are clean along with our actions. Honestly, I don't even have a problem when Bhadra first told me about Maina. I admit I am not happy but neither am I sad. In the end, it is his happiness that is my first priority and getting him forcefully married to another girl just for our caste would gift him lead a happy life? At some point in his life, he would blame me for forcing him and if things don't work out, he would lead a dissatisfied life.

Rohan was stunned.

He questioned:
So you were not against Bhadra's relation because of the caste? But, Madhuri was telling me that you were worried about what our relatives would say and everything. All three of us believed that you were against it because of the caste. What are you saying now doesn't match? Are you serious?

Rohan's mother admitted:
I was initially worried about what our relatives might say but that was no reason for the disagreement. I doubted if she would be happy with Bhadra. I know my son. He is not always calm and pleasant. After marriage, things would

change and if she is not ready she would have to suffer. If she can't handle a word from me, she would be surprised to listen to her husband in the future as men become very different from whom they were before marriage.

Rohan exclaimed:
This was very unexpected I must admit. So what is the answer to my question?

His mother answered:
As I said earlier, my answer would always be marrying the girl of the same caste marriage but if you love a girl, don't fool yourself marrying someone for the sake of caste as it would be betraying yourself. Nothing would be worse.

CHAPTER XXI

Scene XXI

[This scene takes place in Neelkanth's apartment late at night. Rohan knocks on Neelkanth's door, both of them smile looking at each other and Neelkanth welcomes Rohan. The climate was still cloudy and the cold breeze still enriched the atmosphere.]

Looking at Rohan, Neelkanth said:
Isn't it your bedtime? What are you doing here? Did you read the drama I sent you through Mounia? If that is the case, I must apologize beforehand for whatever I have written. I know the scenes seem incomplete. Over the week, I thought about it and I am having second thoughts about the drama.

Rohan entered the flat and sitting down on the sofa in the living room, he said:
I read it and as much as I hate to admit, it is good. I don't think the scenes are incomplete; they are what they should be. They might seem incomplete, the first time a reader reads them but I think they are enough to complete the plot. This would be your best work to date Neelkanth.

Neelkanth asked:
But, I was planning to write a few more scenes between Bhadra and Maina. A few more scenes about Pratyusha and Chandini, what would you say about that?

Rohan thought about it for a moment before saying:

I was thinking about what title this drama should be given and I came up with “Strange Lives”. When I read the drama for the second time, I realized that the characters have been complete because every scene written in the drama symbolizes the turn in their thought to a new perspective. When Maina and her sister talked, it was the inception to the change that Maina was to go through to get back with Bhadra but what I did understand is that it was the inception for the new approach through which Maina viewed her life. The same thing happened with my brother, Pratyusha, Madhuri including myself. I understood that it is not the whole story that is necessary but the scenes that change the perception of characters which would help these characters.

Neelkanth did realize that his drama made good sense in that aspect. He asked:
Then, why is it named Strange Lives? What makes the title appropriate? I was thinking about something more lively. Something that would push the audience to understand what we are trying to sell them.

Rohan pointed out:
Throughout the story, did you notice that our characters interact with their family members and these family members are the root cause for their change? That is nothing strange but what is strange is that these family members have never been in the position that our characters were. Pratyusha’s aunt never had a breakup, Maina’s sister did not master the art of life neither did my mother ever oppose inter-caste marriages. However, these family members help our characters understand that life is perfectly alright and what is wrong is that we are just seeing

it from the wrong perspective.

Neelkanth agreed:
Strange Lives. That would be the title of this drama...

Rohan interrupted saying:
I have one condition for publishing it, only if you promise me that you would come back to work along with me in the publishing company, I would agree to publish this. I think we were really good working together on the manuscripts and the last time I asked you to leave, I admit I was angry and foolish and it was my fault. Please come back and work with me.

Neelkanth thought about the offer for a moment before saying:
I prefer not to come back, Rohan. It was a fantastic experience working with you but that is past, I am sorry but I cannot come back.

Rohan stood up and without saying another word, he left. Just before he was about to get down the steps, both of them hugged.

Rohan said:
It was delightful working with you brother. Always remember that you can always join along whenever you want to.

Neelkanth replied:
Thank you.

About Team

1. **R. S. Chintalapati**
   Contributor

   Ravi is the founder of the community and he writes flash fiction & short stories. His works can be accessed at writerspouch.com/profile/2

2. **Tarun Chintam**
   Editor

   Tarun has been a member of the community since 2017 and he edits short stories and novels. His edited works can be accessed at writerspouch.com/profile/29

3. **Pankaj Tottada**
   Photographer

   Pankaj has been a member of the community since 2015 and he has contributed numerous photographs. His contributions can be accessed at writerspouch.com/profile/13

About Community

Writers Pouch is an Indian community that commissions various works of different art forms. Encompassing creators, contributors, editors, proofreaders, reviewers, photographers, and illustrators, the organisation aims to create unique forms of art in every genre.

Established in 2009, Writers Pouch started by publishing short stories, essays and poems. Later on, the organisation even started releasing novelettes, novellas, novels, book series, & non-fiction.

The goal of Writers Pouch is to explore art uniquely and this is accomplished by commissioning a group of artists on every project. They are a home for all creative individuals who are striving to tell their stories or ideas creatively while holding on to their principles.

If you loved our works, visit our website at writerspouch.com to buy our other titles.

1. I'm Your Loving Intern [2015]
2. Loving Intern [2016]
3. The Soul Snatchers [2016]

9 798885 552172

Printed by Libri Plureos GmbH in Hamburg, Germany